Walking Home to Rosie Lee

BY **A. LaFaye**

illustrated by

KEITH D. SHEPHERD

WAR'S OVER. Government say we free.
Folks be on the move. Getting the feel for freedom.
Not me. I'm looking for my mama, Rosie Lee.
   Master Turner sold my mama away from me.
Haven't seen her since they put me in the fields to
work, but I 'member how she smell like jasmine
flowers in the summer sun.

SHE'S PROBABLY HEADING for freedom like every other body on the road. They walk all day, singing songs, telling stories, and dream-talking of the lives they're gonna live now that they're free. Mr. Gary gonna get him a job on the railroad, laying track.

Yancy's looking for them three brothers he's always telling me about. Miss Sherona wants to be a teacher in one of them new schools you see cropping up like cotton in any old place you can put up a chalkboard and sit yourself down with a book.

THESE FOLKS have freedom on their minds and they talk it out over the nighttime fires that light up their faces like lanterns—all hope and hurry on.

Me, I got my mama, Rosie Lee, on my mind. Can almost see her bright gray eyes, smiling back at me when she'd walk to the fields in the morning.

Papa used to say Mama could bake a pie so sweet, the birds flew out of the sky to have them a taste. Then Papa took sick and left this here world.

All day, all night, I'm looking for folks I don't know, asking if they've heard of my mama, Rosie Lee.

I TELL THEM how Mama always wore a scarf 'round her
neck to hide the scar from being dragged for trying to run free.
    When I thought on it at night, I'd put my hands around my
neck, stare up at the North Star like it might be the eye of God
Himself and pray Mama be all right. Be looking for me. And
finding me 'fore too long.

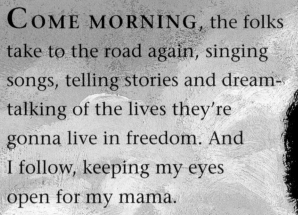

COME MORNING, the folks take to the road again, singing songs, telling stories and dream-talking of the lives they're gonna live in freedom. And I follow, keeping my eyes open for my mama.

Days pass into weeks and one gray evening as Mr. Dark laid down his coat, I see a woman with a yellow scarf 'round her neck as bright as a star. I run up to grab her hand, saying, "Mama?"

But her eyes aren't gray when she looks down at me with a baby child in her arms, saying, "Who's your mama, son?"

"Miss Rosie Lee from the Turner Place, down Mobile way."

"Well, I'm Miss Viola from over near Huntsville."

"You know a Rosie Lee?"

"No, son, I don't, but you could walk with me and Little John."

SHE RUBBED MY HEAD as we kept walking. "Had a
boy named Robert 'bout your age, once."

Slept by Miss Viola and her Little John that night, wishing she
be my Rosie Lee and her probably wishing I be her Robert. But we
can't be. So 'fore Mr. Dark lifted up his coat, I took to the road.

By morning, folks had joined me, singing songs, telling stories—
and dream-talking of the lives they're gonna live in freedom.

WALKED MY WAY through one month, then another. Never heard word of Mama, but I heard talk of the Freedman's Bureaus where they help folks find their kin.

Found such a place looking about as worn out and tired as me. But they didn't have pictures on the wall, just words. Just blasted letters I couldn't read.

"Looking for someone?" asked a lady.

"Yes, ma'am, looking for my mama."

She read about this mama looking for five children and that mama looking for two, right on down the line, each mama searching just as hard for her children as I searched for my mama. But I didn't find Mama on that wall, so the lady took me outside and drew me a picture map to find the next bureau.

COME DUSK, I heard dogs
barking and baying. Figured a
planter turned those dogs on
me, so I set to running. Didn't
get far 'fore those dogs had me
treed like a bear. Kept me there
till Mr. Dark walked through.

Saw a lantern bobbing over
the field and felt sick, sure
I'd been caught.

But it turned out to be
a sharecropper. Holding
that lantern up, he asked,
"You hungry, son? Come
on down and have
some supper."

HADN'T HAD me a sit-down meal for a month of Sundays, felt like picking up the plate and licking it, but Miss Betty, the sharecropper's wife, just kept giving me another little slice of cornbread.

Tried to stop eating, but the hole in my belly wouldn't let me. I told them about my mama's sweet pies. Just then, a lady came to borrow a little something. Hearing me, she said, "Did you say Rosie?"

"Rosie Lee," I said, swallowing the last slice of cornbread whole.

"**THERE'S A ROSIE** who cooks for
the Carters over the Tennessee line."
  She 'bout had me ready to run for Tennessee right then, but
Miss Betty and her husband, Mr. Ray, said I had to have a bath
and a good night's sleep 'fore I found my mama.
  I got clean enough, but couldn't sleep a wink. Got up to fetch
Miss Betty her morning pail of water and cut a log or two for
Mr. Ray to thank them for supper, then headed out after Miss
Dawn done cheered up the sky.

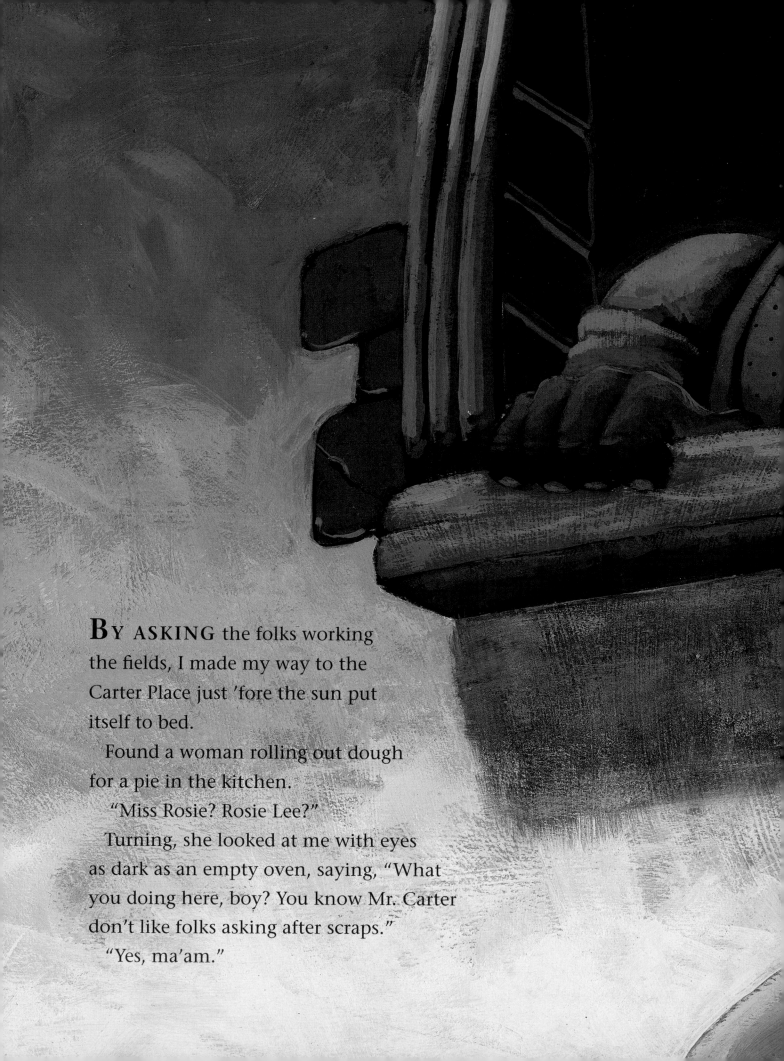

BY ASKING the folks working
the fields, I made my way to the
Carter Place just 'fore the sun put
itself to bed.

Found a woman rolling out dough
for a pie in the kitchen.

"Miss Rosie? Rosie Lee?"

Turning, she looked at me with eyes
as dark as an empty oven, saying, "What
you doing here, boy? You know Mr. Carter
don't like folks asking after scraps."

"Yes, ma'am."

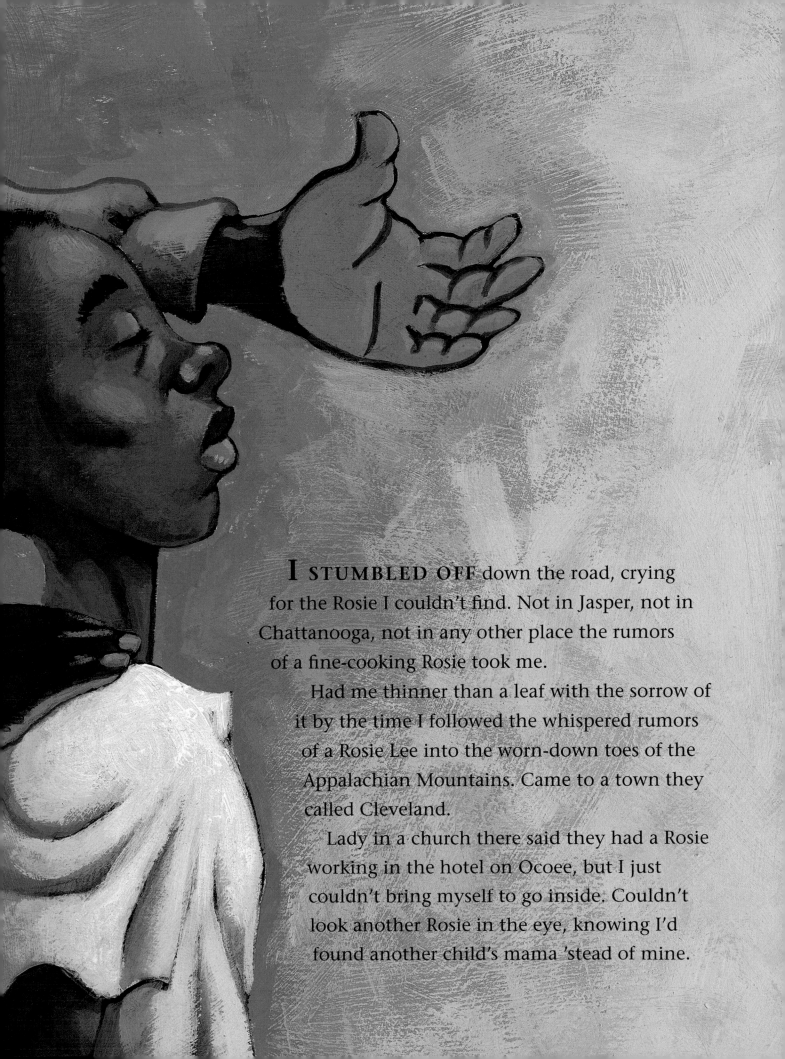

I STUMBLED OFF down the road, crying
for the Rosie I couldn't find. Not in Jasper, not in
Chattanooga, not in any other place the rumors
of a fine-cooking Rosie took me.

Had me thinner than a leaf with the sorrow of
it by the time I followed the whispered rumors
of a Rosie Lee into the worn-down toes of the
Appalachian Mountains. Came to a town they
called Cleveland.

Lady in a church there said they had a Rosie
working in the hotel on Ocoee, but I just
couldn't bring myself to go inside. Couldn't
look another Rosie in the eye, knowing I'd
found another child's mama 'stead of mine.

FROM A TREE on the hill, I watched them ladies in the hotel kitchen stirring pots and cutting this or rolling out that. Then I saw a lady setting out pies in a window, reaching out with a scarf as white as jasmine right there 'round her neck. Near 'bout fell out of that tree for trying to get down.

RAN THERE so fast, left my breath on the hill.
Stood there panting and praying as the lady brought
another pie through the window.

"Mama?" I whispered, afraid it couldn't be true.

Woman dropped a pie right in the dirt. "Gabe?"

Eyes as gray as a kitten's belly. "Mama!"

"Gabe!" she cried, looking like she's gonna climb out that
window to me, but she jumped back into the room.
I could see her running, hear her shouting, "Gabe!"

I TORE AROUND the corner, meeting her racing down the steps and she's hugging me and kissing me and I'm hugging and kissing back, smelling all that sweet jasmine, the both of us just thanking the Good Lord for bringing us home to each other.

That night, I slept snuggled up tight with my mama, praying for all those boys like me searching for their mamas who be searching for them. May each and every one of them find their way home.

Author's Note

AS THE CIVIL WAR CAME TO A CLOSE, many African American children had brothers, sisters, mothers, and fathers who had been sold to other plantations, sometimes far away. A lot of families took to the road to find these relatives. Some people found their loved ones after months, even years, of searching. Many others, though, were never reunited.

I wanted to tell the story of one such family. I wanted readers to understand the journey that so many African Americans embarked upon to find their way home to each other. I addressed this same subject in a novel, *Stella Stands Alone*. When I was doing the research for *Stella*, I came across story after story of the heroic efforts of African Americans to reunite families torn apart by slavery, to build schools, and to gain the rights they deserved to live, work, and raise their own children. I found these stories by scouring through newspapers, diaries, articles, interviews, and books, but the place where I couldn't find them was in picture books for children.

I wrote *Walking Home to Rosie Lee* to celebrate the strength, love, and determination it took for families to find each other at the end of the Civil War. I also wrote it to start filling the historical gap in children's literature that should be overflowing with a wide variety of such stories.

For more on this amazing chapter in our nation's history, please take a look at *From Slavery to Freedom* by John Hope Franklin and Alfred A. Moss, Jr. I'd also encourage you to visit African American history museums like the long overdue Smithsonian National Museum of African American History and Culture which you can visit online at www.nmaac.si.edu.

TO ADIA who found her way home to me. I love you, Moon Baby.
Thank you, God, for bringing us together. —Alexandria

TO MY GRANDMOTHER who always gave me art supplies when I was a child
and said, "Ya'll leave my baby be and let him draw somethin'." —K. D. S.

Visit us at www.cincopuntos.com or call 1-915-838-1625.

Book and cover design by
Vicki Trego Hill of El Paso, Texas.
Printed in Hong Kong by
Creative Printing.

Walking Home to Rosie Lee. Copyright © 2011 by A. LaFaye. Illustrations copyright © 2011 by Keith Darrell Shepherd. All rights reserved. No part of this book may be used or reproduced in any manner whatsoever without written permission except in case of brief quotations for reviews. For information, write Cinco Puntos Press, 701 Texas, El Paso, TX 79901 or call (915) 838-1625. Printed in Hong Kong.
FIRST EDITION   10 9 8 7 6 5 4 3 2 1
Library of Congress Cataloging-in-Publication Data. LaFaye, A. Walking home to Rosie Lee / by A. LaFaye; illustrated by Keith D. Shepherd. — 1st ed.   p. cm.   Summary: At the end of the Civil War, young Gabe meets many other former slaves who are getting a feel for freedom. Their kindness helps him in his quest to find his mother, who was sold away.   ISBN 978-1-933693-97-2 (alk. paper)   [1. Freedmen—Fiction. 2. Voyages and travels—Fiction. 3. Mothers and sons—Fiction. 4. African Americans—Fiction. 5. United States History—1865-1898 Fiction.] I. Shepherd, Keith D., ill. II. Title. PZ7.L1413Wal 2011 [E]—dc22 2010037397